Baggy Brown started out very well indeed. He was made with 999 others just like himself as a Special Limited Edition costing £499.99 each.

In his ear was a golden button in the shape of a crown. Do you know why that was?

Because Baggy Brown was made to celebrate the first birthday of her Royal Highness Princess Sophinyiniannia, first-born and daughter to the King and Queen of Thingland.

First published in 2007
by Hodder Children's Books.

Copyright © Mick Inkpen 2007

Hodder Children's Books
338 Euston Road, London NW1 3BH

Hodder Children's Books Australia
Level 17/207 Kent Street, Sydney, NSW 2000

A catalogue record of this book is
available from the British Library.

ISBN: 978 0 340 93230 8 (HB)
ISBN: 978 0 340 93231 5 (PB)
10 9 8 7 6 5 4 3 2 1

Printed in China

Hodder Children's Books is a
division of Hachette Children's Books,
an Hachette Livre UK Company

Baggy Brown
Mick Inkpen

Hodder
Children's
Books

A division of Hachette Children's Books

Princess Sophinyiniannia, (Sophie for short), also started out well, as you can imagine.

To give you some idea, this is just the top of the pile of cuddly toys that arrived for her the very day she was born.

But do you know, not one of them could stop her crying. Week after week her little howls rang right royally throughout the palace.

In fact her cries were so upsetting that the King and Queen had to pull their crowns over their ears!

At this time Baggy Brown was not called Baggy Brown at all, but just No.1, which was the number stamped on the little gold crown in his ear.

He was the first of the 1000 special bears and the only one, *the only one*, without a price tag. He was priceless, you see, because he was to be presented to Princess Sophie.

And because of this he had a large NOT FOR SALE label slapped on the end of his nose.

Ouch!

It was such a shock that Baggy Brown did not line himself up properly when the big grabbler came round. It missed him completely!

While all the other bears were grabbled and whizzed away, No.1 continued along the conveyor belt and fell straight off the end.

Down he fell, down, down, and back into the very innards of the big red teddy bear machine at Better Bears Ltd.

He was grubbed and fluffed
and plumped and scrodged
and frizzled and squidged
and pummelled and hooshed
and hooshed
and hooshed again!
And when it had finished with
him, the big red teddy bear machine
spat him out onto the factory floor,
where a passing factory worker
called Jack trod on him.

Now Jack wasn't to know that Baggy Brown was a priceless bear. He certainly didn't look like one. So he picked him up and took him home for his young son, Alfie.

Alfie loved Baggy Brown from the moment he saw him. He loved his lopsided face and his soft, saggy body. He loved, too, the strange gold button under Baggy Brown's squashed ear, even though he could make no sense of the name on it.

'No. . . 1?' read Alfie slowly. 'No one is a silly name for a bear.' And he began to think of a proper name.

For three days Alfie carried Baggy Brown everywhere with him. But on the fourth day he hid him, and I will tell you why.

On that day the television news finished with a story about a missing royal bear. 'Number One, first in a long line of bears, is missing!' said the reporter. He was holding up No.2 bear.

'Number One! No.1! That's you Baggy Brown!' said Alfie.

And that is why, almost as soon as Baggy Brown got his real name, he was being stuffed head first into one of Jack's smelly old wellies.

That night Alfie couldn't sleep.
He crept downstairs and
rescued Baggy Brown from
the stair cupboard. Silently he opened
the front door and stepped out into
the cool night.

Alfie knew his way through all
the narrow alleyways that led down
to the banks of The Great River.
He knew too all the watery places
where the coal barges slopped
against the wharves. And he knew
exactly which boat would head off
into the city before first light.

It was into this that he
jumped, curled himself into
a ball around Baggy Brown,
and fell asleep.

Baggy Brown was wide awake as the barge slipped out into The Great River.

He was awake as it slid under black bridges and winking stars.

He was awake as it sounded its horn, just as it always did when approaching the Royal Palace to drop off its load of coal for the Royal Boiler House.

But all the while Alfie slept on.

Which is how he was found by the Royal Stoker. The Stoker, who did not have a clue what to do with the grubby little boy and his grubby little bear, summoned a Royal Footman.

'This belongs to the Princess!' said Alfie holding up Baggy Brown.

The Stoker and the Footman burst into laughter.

'I don't think so, son,' said the Stoker.

'Don't be ridiculous!' said the Footman. 'And take that disgusting object away!'

But Alfie refused to budge.
'It does!' he said.
'It belongs to the Princess!'
So the Footman sent for one of
the Ladies in Waiting.

Lady Jane Farque-Hurrah
was undaunted by the smell
of old welly rising from
Baggy Brown. And having
five children of her own,
she knew exactly when a
child was telling the truth.

She examined Baggy
Brown closely. As she lifted
his coal black ear there was a
bright glint of gold.

'Aha!' she said, and read aloud,
'No.1!'

'His name is Baggy Brown,'
said Alfie.

After a quick clean up with Lady Jane Farque-Hurrah's hanky, Alfie was led through the Palace to the Royal Nursery where Princess Sophie was howling as usual.

Sophie looked at Alfie.
She looked at Baggy Brown.
She stopped crying!
And for the first time in fifty-three weeks the Royal Palace was quiet.

Sadly Alfie pushed Baggy Brown through the bars of the Royal Cot and was led away. But at this moment Sophie started to howl even louder than before!

'Alfie,' whispered Lady Jane, 'it's not Baggy Brown that Sophie wants. . .

. . . it's you!'

So that sealed it. Alfie was allowed to keep Baggy Brown, which of course meant that Baggy Brown was allowed to keep Alfie.

And what about Sophie?
Well the following week a parcel arrived for Alfie. In it was a silver phone with just one golden  button. From that day on, whenever he liked, Alfie could call for the Royal Barge to take him and his friends up The Great River to the Royal Palace to visit Sophie.

This is them in the treehouse that the King had built in the Palace Garden when Sophie was five and Alfie was nine.

And if I had longer to tell you what happened, I would tell you that Sophie loved Alfie and his baggy brown bear for the rest of her life, and married him just after her 21st birthday.

I would tell you that Alfie's father, Jack, became the proud owner of Better Bears Ltd, but his proudest day was the day he learned that his grandson, future King of Thingland, was to be named after him.

I would tell you that on the day His Royal Highness Prince Jack was born, 10,000 bears rolled off the conveyor belt at Better Bears Ltd. . .

. . . and I would tell you that
none of them was loved as
much as Baggy Brown.

Other books by Mick Inkpen:

One Bear at Bedtime
The Blue Balloon
Threadbear
Billy's Beetle
Penguin Small
Lullabyhullaballoo!
Nothing
Bear
The Great Pet Sale

Kipper
Kipper's Toybox
Kipper's Birthday
Kipper's Book of Counting
Kipper's Book of Colours
Kipper's Book of Opposites
Kipper's Book of Weather
Where, Oh Where, is Kipper's Bear?
Kipper's Snowy Day
Kipper's Christmas Eve
Kipper's A to Z
Kipper and Roly
Kipper's Monster
Kipper's Balloon
Kipper's Beach Ball
One Year with Kipper

The Little Kipper series
The Little Kipper Collection
Kipper Story Collection
The 2nd Little Kipper Collection
The Mick Inkpen Treasury

Everyone Hide from Wibbly Pig
In Wibbly's Garden
Wibbly Pig Board Books
Is It Bedtime Wibbly Pig?
Tickly Christmas Wibbly Pig
Wibbly Pig's Silly Big Bear

Blue Nose Island:
Ploo and the Terrible Gnobbler
Beachmoles and Bellvine
Bokobikes